FOR MORGAN'S GRANDPA

PAT HUTCHINS

NIGHT

A TRUMPET CLUB SPECIAL EDITION

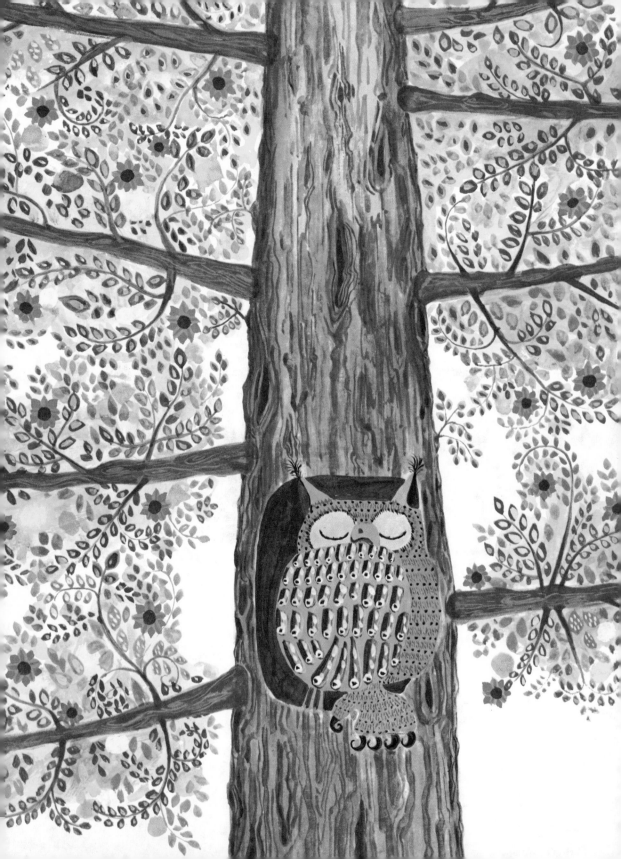

Owl tried to sleep.

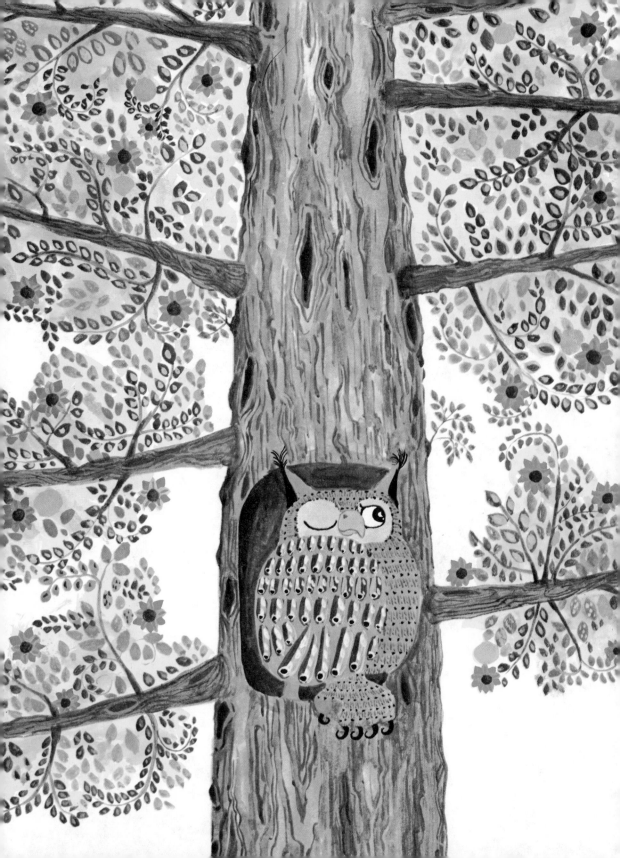

The bees buzzed,
buzz buzz,
and Owl tried to sleep.

The squirrel cracked nuts,
crunch crunch,
and Owl tried to sleep.

The crows croaked,
caw caw,
and Owl tried to sleep.

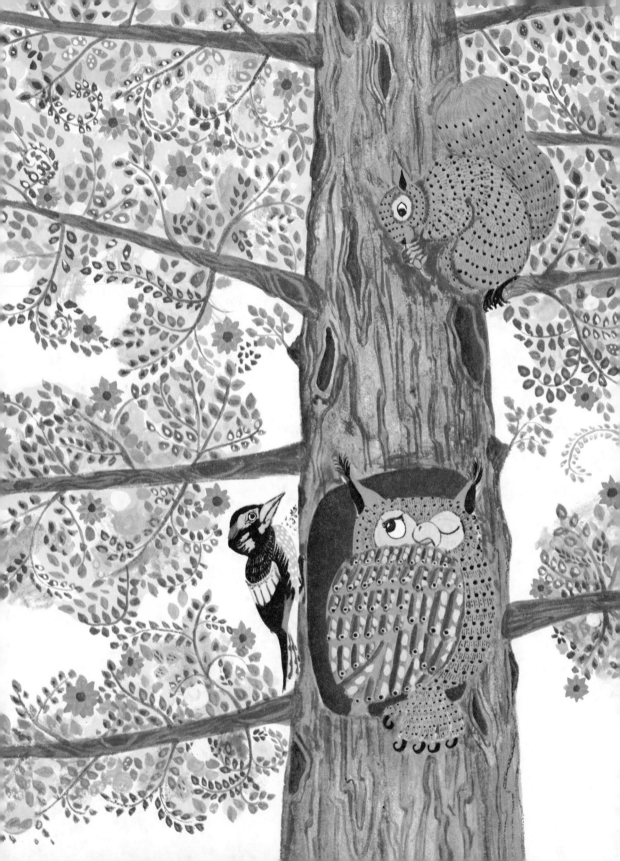

The woodpecker pecked,
rat-a-tat! rat-a-tat!
and Owl tried to sleep.

The starlings chittered,
twit-twit, twit-twit,
and Owl tried to sleep.

The jays screamed,
ark ark,
and Owl tried to sleep.

The cuckoo called,
cuckoo cuckoo,
and Owl tried to sleep.

The robin peeped,
pip pip,
and Owl tried to sleep.

The sparrows chirped,
cheep cheep,
and Owl tried to sleep.

The doves cooed,
         croo croo,
and Owl tried to sleep.

The bees buzzed, buzz buzz.
The squirrel cracked nuts,
crunch crunch.
The crows croaked, caw caw.
The woodpecker pecked,
rat-a-tat! rat-a-tat!
The starlings chittered,
twit-twit, twit-twit.
The jays screamed, ark ark.
The cuckoo called,
cuckoo cuckoo.
The robin peeped, pip pip.
The sparrows chirped,
cheep cheep.
The doves cooed, croo croo,
and Owl couldn't sleep.

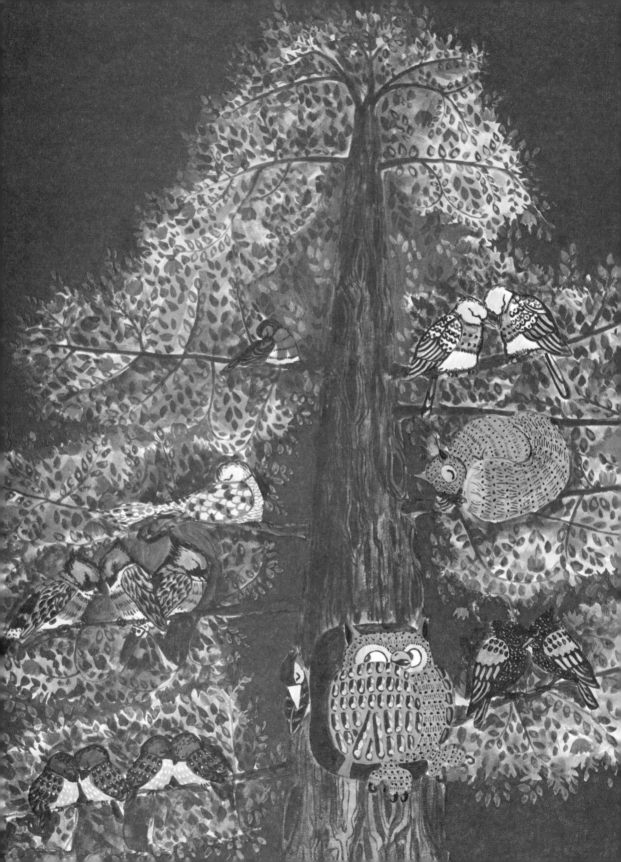

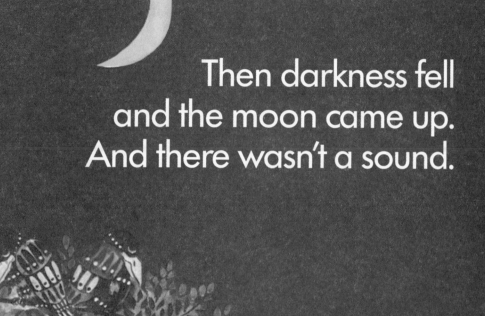

Then darkness fell
and the moon came up.
And there wasn't a sound.

Owl screeched,
screech screech,
and woke everyone up.

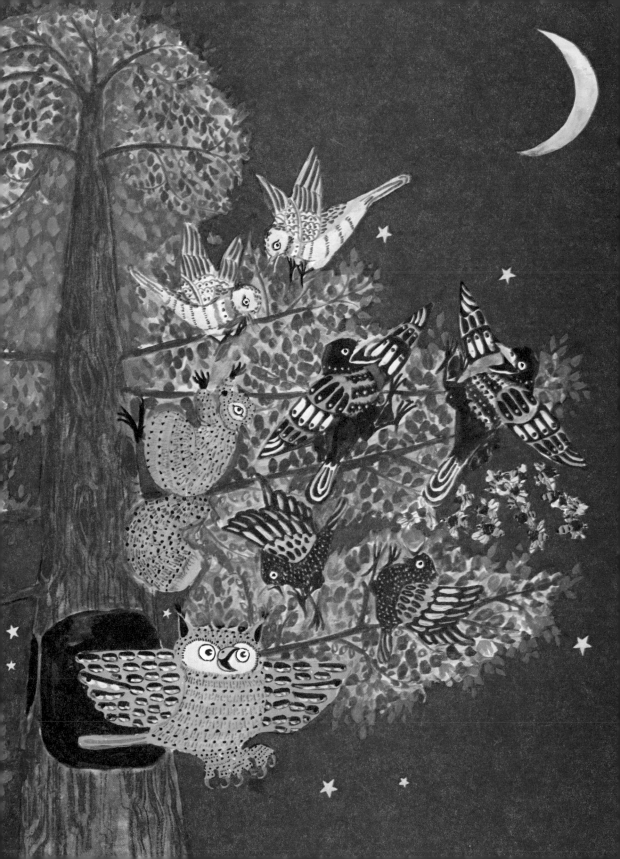

Published by The Trumpet Club
1540 Broadway, New York, New York 10036

ISBN: 0-440-84508-4

This edition published by arrangement with
Macmillan Publishing Company
Printed in the United States of America
October 1991

10 9 8 7 6 5 4 3 2
UPC